BUTTER CHUCK

Written By Amanda Kleback
Illustrated and Original Character
by Nikki Roquet

To: Delainey Bell
For shedding her homemade butterfly wings for those of angels.
N.R. and A.K.

This is Butter Chuck.

He is not an ordinary woodchuck.
He dreams to be a butterfly.

He dances, plays, and tends to the neighborhood flowers, just like the butterflies do.

Other woodchucks made fun of him.
In fact, that's how he got his name.

One night, after a tough day of taunting and caring for flowers, Butter Chuck looked wishfully into the night sky. He wanted to be a butterfly so he could just fly away. With tattered wings made of old leaves and broken sticks on his back, he fell asleep.

Moments later, Butter Chuck was awoken by a rustling sound behind him. He slowly opened his eyes. He was not in the tree stump he called home. Oh no, he was in the most beautiful place he had ever seen.

Flowers of all colors towered over the little woodchuck.

He saw giant butterflies all around him filling their water cans with drops of dew.

In amazement, Butter Chuck just watched until he felt a soft wing on his shoulder.

The wing was from the most enchanting of all butterflies. She said to him, "Welcome Butter Chuck, we are happy you came to visit."

Butter Chuck sighed and put his head down.
He said, "But I am not a beautiful butterfly, I do not belong here. I do not belong anywhere."

The butterfly lifted Butter Chuck's chin and said to him, "Butter Chuck, you are the most beautiful butterfly of all. You belong here and anywhere else you want to be. You ARE Butter Chuck."

With those words of kindness, they shared a magical hug. And when they let go, Butter Chuck found himself back in his bed, in the tree stump he called home.

The morning's sun warmed Butter Chuck's front stoop as he peered out. He was not surrounded by magical butterflies and giant flowers; just the small blooms he tended to everyday.

He grabbed his watering can and went to work. And like all of the other days, the others started to taunt him.

But today was different.
He turned to them and said, "I AM Butter Chuck."
Just as he said those proud words, a beautiful set of butterfly wings spread behind him.

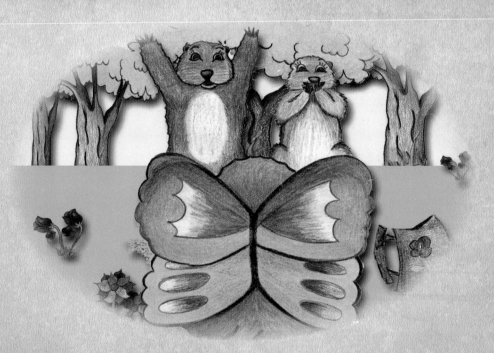

The others smiled as they watched something special.

Butter Chuck stood tall as he smiled.
With his wings spread proudly he said,
"I AM BUTTER CHUCK!"
He was very happy to be himself.